JENNIFER NORTHWAY has written and illustrated a number of acclaimed picture books. *Get Lost, Laura!* was shortlisted for the Smarties Award. In addition to her own stories, Jennifer has illustrated books for many well-known authors, including Jill Paton Walsh, Floella Benjamin and Mary Hoffman. Her book with Mary Hoffman, *Nancy No-Size*, was also shortlisted for the Smarties Award. Her work has been televised in England and all over Europe on children's programmes, and in New Zealand and Australia. She wrote and illustrated *See You Later, Mum*, also published by Frances Lincoln.

For Mike and Amy – J.N.

Text and illustrations copyright © Jennifer Northway 1993
The right of Jennifer Northway to be identified as the author of this work has been asserted by
her in accordance with the Copyright, Designs and Patents Act, 1988 (United Kingdom).

This edition published in Great Britain in 2008 by
Frances Lincoln Children's Books, 4 Torriano Mews,
Torriano Avenue, London NW5 2RZ
www.franceslincoln.com

British Library Cataloguing in Publication Data available on request

ISBN 978-1-84507-897-3

Printed in Singapore

1 3 5 7 9 8 6 4 2

Get Lost, Laura!

Jennifer Northway

F

FRANCES LINCOLN
CHILDREN'S BOOKS

Lucy and her cousin Alice were dressing up.

"Let's play 'Going to the Ball'," said Lucy.

"I'm in the carriage already," said Alice, swinging on the garden gate.

"Quick, get on!"

As Lucy wobbled to the gate in Mum's high
pointy shoes Laura caught hold of her heel.
"I want them!" she said.

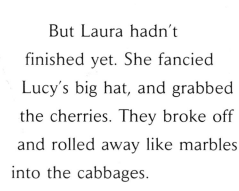

"Oh, push off, Laura," said Lucy crossly, but she gave the shoes to her little sister.

She put on a green pair instead. Then Laura wanted them too.

"How many feet do you think you've got?" sighed Lucy, handing them over. "Why don't you go and play in the sandpit."

But Laura hadn't finished yet. She fancied Lucy's big hat, and grabbed the cherries. They broke off and rolled away like marbles into the cabbages.

"*Get lost*, Laura!" said Lucy. "*Go away!*"

Laura stuck the big hat on her head. She didn't care a bit.

"I'm fed up with Laura," Lucy hissed to Alice. "Let's hide."

"But your mum says we're to play with her," whispered Alice.

"We can still keep an eye on her," said Lucy, running up the garden on tiptoe.

"Hide and Seek, Laura!" she called.

Alice pulled open the shed door.

"Quick, let's hide," she said.

"Dad doesn't like us coming in here," said Lucy. "He says it's not safe."

"We'll be *very* careful," said Alice.

The shed smelt of paint and damp, and was full of tools and flower pots. They found an old pram they sometimes played with, but they couldn't get it out from behind the junk.

"Look," said Lucy, "there's a big hole in the planks here. Maybe it's a secret passage." They squeezed through and found themselves in next-door's garden.

Lucy's neighbour was sitting in a deckchair reading the paper.

"Is that two cats I see there in my flowerbed?" she asked. "Your daddy needs to mend that hole, Lucy, otherwise *I* might crawl through and give *you* a fright!" But she was smiling.

They wriggled back into the shed. Alice's dress caught on a plank and ripped all the way down one side.

"I'm glad I haven't got a baby sister," said Alice. "Babies are yucky. Always wet and dribbly."

"Laura's all right really," said Lucy, "She's only dribbling because she's getting teeth. Mum'll be cross if she sees we're not playing with her."

She opened the shed door.

"Come and find us, Laura!" she called.

There was a long silence.

"I wonder where she's gone," said Alice. They looked all round the shed, and then under it, but there was no sign of her.

There weren't many other places to look.

Alice pulled all the clothes out of the suitcase.

Lucy looked in the cabbages. They were full of scrunchy snails and slimy slugs, and Laura wasn't under them.

Alice lifted the dustbin lid and peered in, but she shut it again quickly –
even Laura wouldn't hide in *there*!

"She can't have gone far," said Alice. "Her legs are only little."

"She can move really fast when she wants to," said Lucy.
"Oh, Alice! You left the gate open after you were swinging on it!"

There were some boys playing football on the field at the back,
but there was no sign of Laura.

Lucy called over the wall to her other neighbour, Julie.

"Have you seen Laura anywhere?" she asked.

"You didn't leave the gate open, did you?" said Julie. "You'd better go and tell your mum while I check the playing field." She hurried off down the garden.

"Do you think she's really lost?" said Alice. "Monsters or anything might get her."
"I don't believe in monsters," said Lucy bravely. "Maybe she got into the shed
when we came out, and she wants us to find her."

But she wasn't in the shed, and although they wriggled through
the hole again into next-door's flowerbed, she wasn't there either.

Lucy began to panic. In the rush back
through the shed she knocked over
something black and smelly.

"I wish we'd never come in here!" she shouted angrily. "I *said* we shouldn't! It's all *your* fault, Alice!"

"*You're* the one who wanted to hide!" said Alice indignantly.

"Yes, but you were swinging on the gate and didn't shut it!" shouted Lucy.

"She's *your* sister, and *you* shouldn't have left her!" Alice shouted back.

"*I* said we shouldn't. I bet you'll be in big trouble!"

Lucy burst into tears. "Mum'll be furious," she wailed,
"I'll have to run away too!"

    Alice felt a bit sorry then.

"Don't do that," she said, "That'll be two lost instead of one. Anyway it *was* partly my fault. They'll probably say we can't play together ever again." She started crying too.

"I'd better tell Mum now," sniffed Lucy. "I wish I'd never told Laura to get lost."

She pushed open the kitchen door *very* slowly... and there, sitting on Mum's knee, was Laura!

"Laura!" cried Alice, and burst out laughing.
"You were here all the time!"

"Don't say anything cross, Mum," said Lucy, wiping her eyes on Mum's sleeve. "I know we should have been watching her. We looked for her *everywhere*! Sorry."

Laura slid off Mum's lap. She liked the look of Lucy's fancy hairslide, and tried to pull it out of her hair.

"Ow!" shouted Lucy. "Get..."
She *was* going to say, "Get lost, Laura!"

...but she didn't!

MORE LUCY AND ALICE BOOKS BY JENNIFER NORTHWAY FROM FRANCES LINCOLN

LUCY'S RABBIT

Lucy is busy making decorations for her Mum's birthday with the help
of her cousin Alice. When they discover a rabbit eating Dad's pansies
they think it is a great idea for a surprise present.
But keeping the mischievous rabbit out of trouble for long enough
to give her to Mum is much harder than they expect.
And what will Mum say when she sees what her surprise present
has done to her favourite pair of slippers?

ISBN 978-1-84507-895-9

LUCY'S QUARREL

Lucy and her cousin Alice are best friends.
But when Alice calls Lucy bossy it is the start of a big quarrel
that threatens to spoil Lucy's birthday.
Can Lucy and Alice make friends again in time for Lucy's party?

ISBN 978-1-84507-896-6

Frances Lincoln titles are available from all good bookshops.
You can also buy books and find out more about your favourite titles,
authors and illustrators on our website: www.franceslincoln.com